D0239307

THIS WALKER BOOK BELONGS TO:

For Russell, with love J.L.

For James P.C.

First published 1990 by Walker Books Ltd
87 Vauxhall Walk, London SE11 5HJ

This edition published 1992

6 8 10 9 7

Printed in Hong Kong

British Library Cataloguing in Publication Data
A catalogue record for this book is
available from the British Library.
ISBN 0-7445-2030-4

Morag and the Lamb

Written by Joan Lingard

Illustrated by Patricia Casey

"Now be good – both of you!" said Mother.
She drove off leaving Russell and Morag
to stay with Grandma and Grandpa.
"Why does everyone tell us to be
good?" asked Russell. "We *are* good."
Morag barked to show that she agreed.

Grandma said, "It's lambing time."
Grandpa said, "Russell, you must see
that Morag doesn't worry the sheep."
Russell said, "Morag, you *mustn't*
worry the sheep."

The farmer came along the road in
her canary-yellow tractor.
"I'm going to feed the sheep," she said.
"Would you like to come along, Russell?"
"Oh yes, please!" said Russell.
Morag wagged her tail.

“We’d better not take Morag,” said
the farmer. “Just in case she tries to
worry the sheep.”
Russell was puzzled. Why should she
worry sheep? “It’s a serious matter when
dogs worry sheep,” said the farmer.
“If they do, they often have to be
put away.”

Put away?
Russell turned pale.
So did Morag, under her fur.
Russell said, “Morag, you really
must not worry the sheep.”

Grandpa lifted Russell up.
"Hold tight now!" said Grandma.
Morag was left behind.

She went slowly down the garden,
keeping close to the dry-stone wall.
She pricked up her ears. What was that?
"*Baa-aa. Baa-aaa.*"

She jumped over the wall
into the next field.
Then she saw the lamb.

The lamb was all tangled
up in a bramble bush.

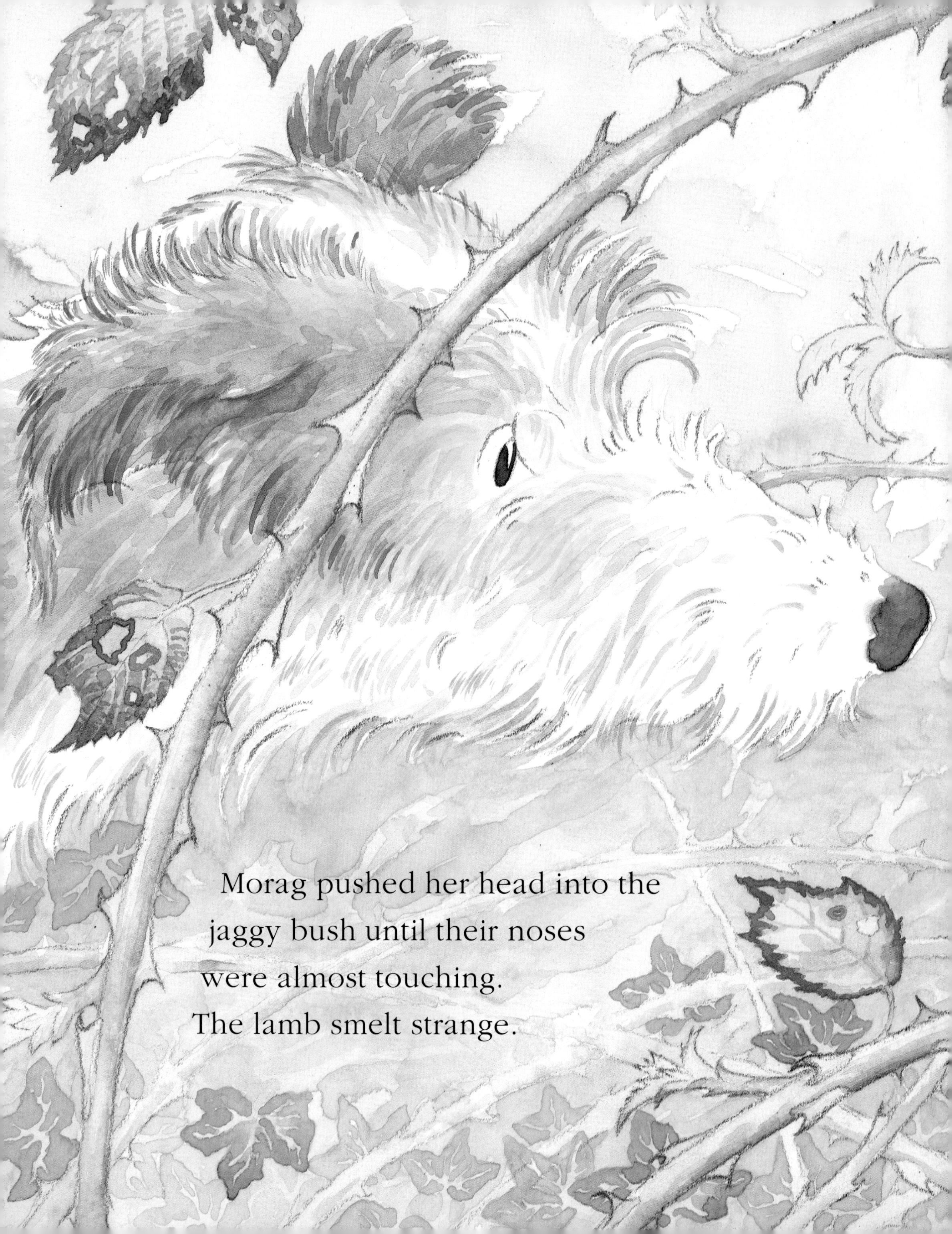

Morag pushed her head into the jaggy bush until their noses were almost touching. The lamb smelt strange.

She wriggled closer and their
noses went bump!
"*Baa-aa-aaa*," cried the lamb.
It looked very worried.

But Morag hadn't worried it, had she?
What would happen if the farmer thought
she had? Would she be put away?
She leapt over a stream and galloped up
the field. The wind rushed in her ears.
She saw Russell.

She barked loudly,

once…

twice…

three times,

telling him to come and follow her.

“Oh, Morag!” said Russell.

Morag looked up at him with anxious eyes. *Had* she worried the lamb?

“We must get help,” said Russell.

“*Baa-aa*,” cried the lamb.

"Come quickly!" Russell yelled.
The farmer began to run down
the field towards them.

"Goodness me!" said the farmer.
"You *are* in a tangle."
She eased aside the branches of the bramble bush and set the lamb free.

"Good boy, Russell!" said the farmer.
"It was Morag who found the lamb,"
said Russell.
"*Very* good girl, Morag," said the farmer.
"Morag didn't worry the lamb, did
she?" asked Russell.
"Of course not!" said the farmer. "To worry
sheep means to chase and try to hurt them."
"Morag would *never, ever* do that,"
said Russell and Morag barked,

once...

twice...

three times...

to show that she agreed.